MORBID DELUSIONS

A COLLECTION OF SPINE-TINGLING SHORT STORIES

MORBID DELUSIONS

A COLLECTION OF
SPINE-TINGLING SHORT STORIES

MICHAEL JULIUS BUCKNER

OMAHA, NEBRASKA

MORBID DELUSIONS:
A Collection of Spine-Tingling Short Stories
Tiny Trilogies of Terror - Vol. 1

Published by Digital Dredz Media
www.DigitalDredzMedia.com

Paperback: 978-1-952986-01-7
Mobi: 978-1-952986-02-4
EPUB: 978-1-952986-03-1
Library of Congress Control Number: 2020910041
Cataloging in Publication Data on file with the Publisher.

Production by Concierge Publishing Services, Omaha, NE
Printed in the United States of America
10 9 8 7 6 5 4 3 2 1

For my dearest wife Raquel,
whose love, patience,
kindness, and strength can
never be measured.
I love you.

CONTENTS

INTRODUCTION

THERE ARE FIVE ESSENTIAL ELEMENTS FOR SURVIVAL: AIR. WARMTH. WATER. FOOD. SEX. THESE ARE OBVIOUS, BUT THERE IS A SIXTH ELEMENT WHICH IS JUST AS IMPORTANT, WITHOUT WHICH, WE CANNOT LIVE.

THAT LAST ESSENTIAL ELEMENT,
MY FRIENDS, IS FEAR.

Think about it. We are all such frail, dependent creatures. It's no wonder that we are so fearful; certain death seemingly lurks at every turn. A few brief moments without air, and we suffocate. It takes just a few minutes to burn, a matter of hours to freeze to death. A few days without water, or a few weeks without food, and our life force dissipates. Keep us from procreating, and in a handful of decades, the entire human race would perish. Fear has gotten us here. Yes, we need fear. It is the engine that pushes us to survive.

Our relationship with fear has been forged in the crucible of evolution. Our ancestors, devoid of fur, claws, swiftness, or flight, were naked and vulnerable to the greatest of nature's predators. Luckily for us, nature endowed humankind with three gifts: opposable thumbs, the driving impulse of fear, and the ability to imagine. We used our minds to survive. We dreamed up the club, the spear, the wheel, and the plow. Yet even in these gifts, existential threats lurked. Desire. Ambition. Envy. Hatred. These feelings brought something new: we began to fear each other.

As society advanced, fear kept us alive. It drove us to improvise weapons, to build shelters, to establish social boundaries, to reshape the future. Once our Neanderthal ancestors had reached a crude balance of power, they sat safely by their campfires at night, yet fear still preyed upon their increasingly sophisticated psyches. The unexplained noise in the brush no longer belonged to the tiger. Instead, men and women began to fear the unpredictable, the unexplained, the abnormal, the supernatural. Our fears became more and more human. The hunchback, the priestess, the cripple, the clairvoyant all earned sacred places among the crowded enclaves of human-kind. The frightened masses told each other eerie myths, ghost stories, and cautionary tales, to protect each other and to try to make sense of the world around them. Today, we are no different. We still hold hands a little tighter in the dark. We huddle together in the wee hours before dawn, and we will, at times, dare to investigate the unexplained shuffle on the outskirts of camp.

❏ ❏ ❏

Yes, fear is still part of our modern lives. In fact, it's been with us so long, we've come to the point where fear has become our friend. When it's not around, we kind of miss it. Therefore, we seek it out. We long to feel it. We find it at haunted houses, in crowded movie theaters, at amusement parks, at festivals.

Be honest. Fear is the reason why you were drawn to this tiny trilogy of macabre and dreadful stories. Because deep inside, along with the air you breathe, and the food you eat, you need fear to make you feel alive. Embrace your fear and revel in it.

Accept these stories then, as a humble offering to the demons lurking within you, to the flitting shadows that writhe at the edges of your vision. May you find the exhilaration of suspense, the luscious twinge of dread, and the delicious chill of fear. May a thousand shivers ripple along your spine. For what good is this gift of life, if we cannot truly live it in all its nightmarish glory?

Omaha, Nebraska
June 19, 2020

IF AN INJURY HAS TO
BE DONE TO A MAN IT
SHOULD BE SO SEVERE
THAT HIS VENGEANCE
NEED NOT BE FEARED.

~NICCOLO MACHIAVELLI

CASUALTY
OF WAR

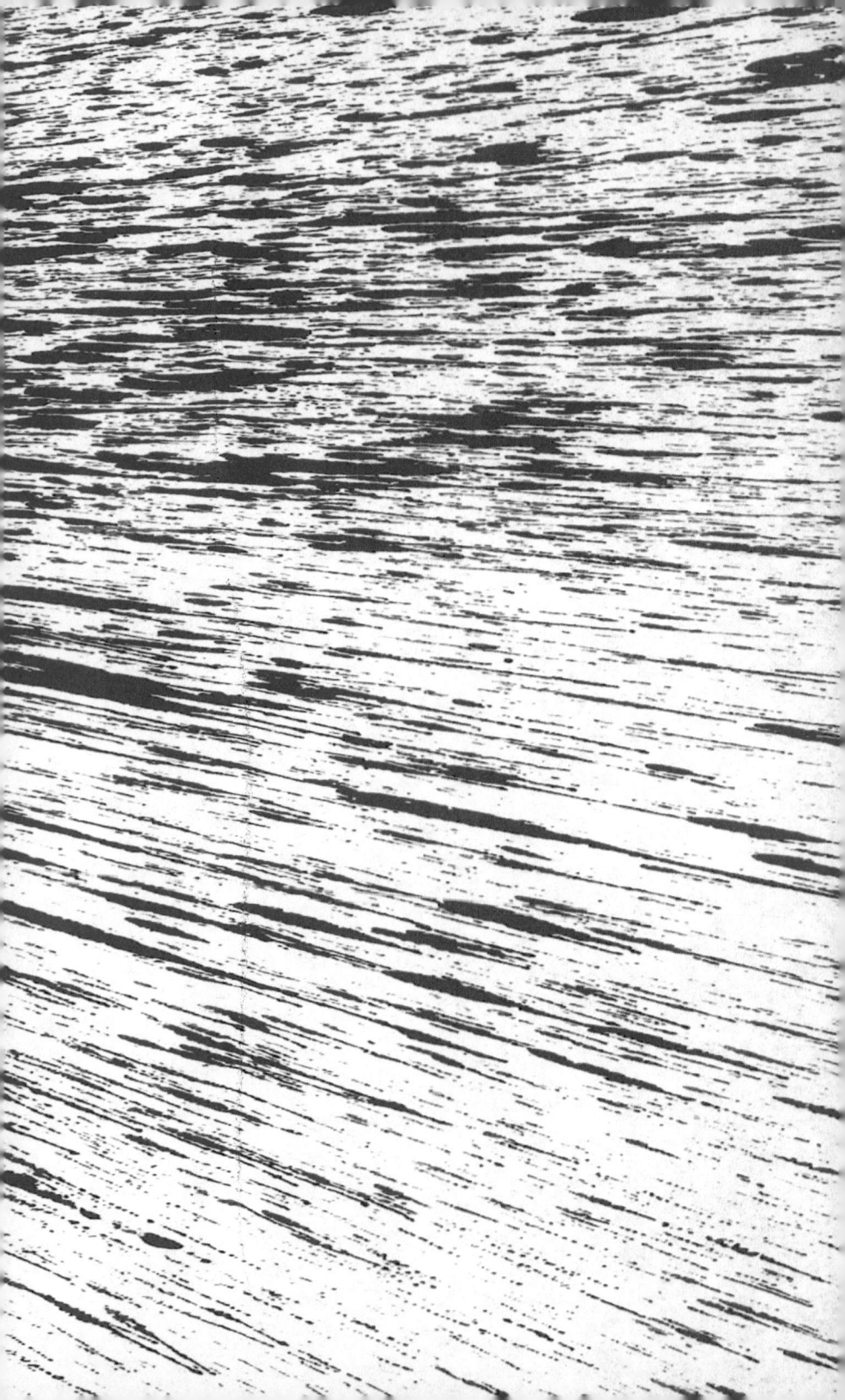

CASUALTY OF WAR

THE DESPERATE BATTLE RAGED OVER THE GREEN HILLS, CHURNED THROUGH THE FERTILE VALLEY BELOW, AND DECIMATED THE SPRAWLING CITY BESIDE THE RIVER. ALL DAY LONG, MEN SCREAMED, BLED, AND DIED, BLASTED APART BY SEARING SCRAPS OF JAGGED METAL.

In time, the fighting ebbed. The sun dropped low along the horizon. Shadows clung to shattered buildings. The invading force had been all but destroyed.

The last of these invaders, Erhard Wulff, a cold, cruel-faced scrap of a man, woke with a start. He lay in a sandbagged trench, now desolate in ruin. His head hurt desperately. His limbs ached. A deep fatigue consumed him. His thoughts swirled in a fog of confusion. The pungent musk of spent gunpowder, and the sour tang of his own sweat clogged his nostrils. Flashes of action rumbled through his mind.

For a moment, he stared into the gloom, listening. He heard footsteps, running, perhaps twenty meters away. Friend or foe? He couldn't tell. Then a voice cried out, followed by the sharp crack of a .32 caliber pistol, the kind favored by the enemy. After a moment, he heard another shot, and another! Closer this time. A wail of agony suddenly rang out from the narrow streets. The cry rose up, morphed into a tragic sob, then faded to nothing. The footsteps tramped off into the distance.

Wulff stared up at the darkening skies. Chills peppered the back of his neck. He knew that he had to move. He wasn't sure he could. His legs felt stiff and heavy. He tried to sit up, but a terrible jolt of pain ripped through his temples, forcing him to lay back again. His thoughts raced. He heard his own breath as he considered the situation. Obviously, the assault had failed. The army Wulff had grown to love had been smashed—humiliated and defeated. If he stayed here, he was surely doomed along with any remaining comrades who had dared to attack this wretched land.

The gunshots had made it clear. There would be no mercy. His only hope was to find a comrade or two, regroup with them, and find a way to leave this place—hopefully together.

As these thoughts occurred to him, he felt a heavier wave of exhaustion. A brief rest, he thought, before setting out. Anyway, his chances would be much better after dark. He eased back into the trench and closed his eyes...

□ □ □

Wulff suddenly sat up, looked around, and realized night had fallen. All was quiet. He climbed to his feet, reaching for the holster on his hip. It was empty. Where was the pistol? He struggled to recall. After a moment, he thought he remembered. In the desperate scrum, he had fired his last shot, then whipped the spent pistol at an enemy soldier. It had hit the man square in the face, and Wulff saw the surprised look in the man's eyes. Blood gushed from the man's nose and he had charged across the short gap between them. Wulff had watched that surprise turn to rage, and then the man was upon him. They had grappled and landed on the ground. What then? The ensuing events were hazy and unclear. Hadn't that been the same enemy fighter who had charged at Heinrich, grenade in hand? No, it was the bearded one, he argued to himself. The one who had slammed a bayonet into poor Emile. Emile had called out to him. Wulff gasped at the thought, and sorrow, like a putrid wave, rose up within him carrying with it the flotsam and debris of war.

When his eyes adjusted to the gloom, he groped about for his rifle. It sat charred and useless on the ground. The trench was littered with the wreckage of battle. Surely something useful remained. Clawing about on hands and knees, he managed to scrounge up a few pistol rounds.

Along with Emile and Heinrich, he and several others had held this position. They had fought off wave after wave of counter-attackers. And for what? He vaguely recalled Emile's screams, an explosion, and that last gory and violent struggle. He now knelt in a hole on a blasted patch of earth at the edge of a ruined town, surrounded by blood and carnage and death. He cursed and spat on the ground. Wulff scanned the trench around him. Had he alone remained? His friends were nowhere to be found. Perhaps they had made it out after all.

Nearby, an enemy soldier, the surprised man, lay there like a discarded slab of rotten meat. The man's gore-smeared uniform was riddled with a dozen shrapnel holes. His face was pale, eyes half open. A faint smile lingered. Wulff stared at him, and for an instant, thought he saw a glimmer of movement in the man's eyes. Wulff shrunk back, ready to fight. Nothing happened. He looked up and saw that the moon now glinted in the night sky. Just a reflection, he concluded with a wry chuckle and a sigh of relief. Resuming his search, Wulff hastily scrounged around near the motionless corpse. His hands fumbled over the cool earth, then closed on the smooth metal of a pistol. It was his. He tested its action. It still worked. Satisfied, he loaded the scavenged rounds, shoved the pistol into his belt, staggered to his feet, and crept from the dank hole.

◻ ◻ ◻

As he staggered along, Wulff surveyed the rubble-strewn streets. Smoldering buildings loomed overhead like rows of upright coffins. A faint stench of damp rot rose from the churned earth. In the distance lay the river and the dark shadows of the hills to which he must return. He crept from shadow to shadow searching for any remnant of his defeated comrades. From somewhere in the darkness, the methodical gunshots disrupted the stillness.

He crept through the rubble until at last he sensed movement ahead... the familiar drag and shuffle of a soldier hauling a wounded comrade through the cobbled streets. From the sound there were at least two, perhaps three. His blood quickened. Were they the comrades he sought, moving toward the brooding hills? He needed to see first, for fear of stumbling upon one of the enemy death squads. He decided to follow from a safe distance until he reached a good vantage point where he could watch unobserved.

Wulff cut through an alley shuffling quietly over desolate piles of rubble. His angle of pursuit drew him nearer, until he finally caught a glimpse of them. He was right—there were two of them, one dragging the other down the street in lurching bursts of motion.

The upright one seemed bizarrely tall and thin, yet somehow familiar. His uniform was tattered and filthy, one ragged bloody sleeve hung empty at his side. With his remaining arm, he dragged the other man along by the collar behind him. He trudged forward steadily, head down, a battered helmet drawn low over his brow. The morbid cadence repeated—limp, drag, limp, drag—as he shuffled past. The mangled figure he dragged was surely dead. Where the man's legs should have been, white struts of bone jutted out at odd angles. A decaying tangle of entrails slopped from its shattered waist. Each time the lurid pair moved forward, little bits of blood and gore spilled onto the road. As Wulff watched this ghoulish pair, his stomach churned. Through the gloom, however, he could not make out whether they were comrades, yet couldn't shake the sense that he knew them. His morbid curiosity piqued; he would watch where the two were headed.

He stepped forward, stumbled, and dislodged a loose brick which clattered along the ground.

The two fetid beings stopped and looked in his direction. He felt the churning revulsion as the one in front lifted its head to reveal a disfigured, half-blasted skull. It moaned, awaking the mangled ghoul at its feet. The limbless ghoul shook loose from the other, and began clawing slowly towards Wulff, dragging itself across the ground with menacing determination.

Wulff recoiled, his mind reeling on the brink of panic. "Mein Gott! Do dead men walk?" He hissed aloud. He raised the pistol and shouted a command to halt. The two ghouls shambled closer. He yelled again at them. They moaned in reply. At last he fired. Bullets slammed home in both ghouls, spraying chunks of gore with each impact. As the echoes of the gunshots died away, the mournful hiss of the two ghouls seemed to rise and swell throughout the deserted canyons of the streets. The two continued their slow, relentless pursuit. He sensed movement to his left and looked. Another ghoul, in rotting fatigues, scrambled from the bowels of a wrecked building. Then another, and another rose from the stinking rubble.

Wulff unleashed his last few rounds. Deadly and precise, the bullets smacked home with soggy thuds. Still the creatures pursued. From mangled limbs to punctured guts, they all displayed wounds that would have killed any normal man. Wulff screamed aloud with rage and despair as madness clawed at his sanity. Are these things not dead? He had delivered several mortal wounds himself, still they drew relentlessly forward. His pistol clicked on empty. He flipped it around and whipped it at a tall ghoul. The pistol tumbled end over end and smacked into the fleshy remains of its face. The monstrosity raised its ruined visage toward Wulff, and it called out to him! In that moment, Wulff wanted to scream, to run, for he thought he saw, embedded in the gory remains, a familiar face, the face of—

At his feet, the crawling ghoul snarled and dug its bony nails into his shin. Wulff fought to free himself. The other ghouls crowded upon him. He was surrounded. No room to run. He lashed out at the horde. Their slimy claws reached for him, seized him. Their chilling grip tightened. They overwhelmed him, and forced him to the ground. Their plaintive moans echoed in his ears, bathed his mind, drained his will to fight, and then somehow, calmed his fears.

A deep guttural hissing blended into the sympathetic and eerie hum of a long forgotten lullaby. The blathering horde swept him from the ground, and lifted him up, carrying him upon their shoulders in a macabre funeral procession.

He looked again at the fiends who conveyed him. Their clothes were tattered, blood-stained, yet familiar. The faces, also bloodied, shredded, yet somehow recognizable. Heinrich? Emile? Yes, now he remembered. They had crouched in the trench as the enemy charged in, grenade in hand. Heinrich surged forward to meet him, then flopped to the ground on top of the grenade. Emile, kneeling in his own slippery guts, called out. He bent to help Emile. Then a loud blast rocked the ground. The shrapnel felt hot, sharp, intolerable.

Wulff felt a terrible and chilling realization. He belonged with them. He slowly reached up towards his own brow. The bone was hopelessly shattered; the back of his head an empty void. He stared at his trembling fingertips, smeared with the rotted jelly of his mortal wounds. At last, with a tortured sigh, he lay back in acceptance, his own lament blending in with the mournful haunting wail of those who bore him toward oblivion.

THERE ARE THINGS
WHICH A MAN IS AFRAID
TO TELL EVEN TO
HIMSELF, AND EVERY
DECENT MAN HAS A
NUMBER OF SUCH
THINGS STORED AWAY
IN HIS MIND.

~FYODOR DOSTOEVSKY

RUN, FRANK! RUN!

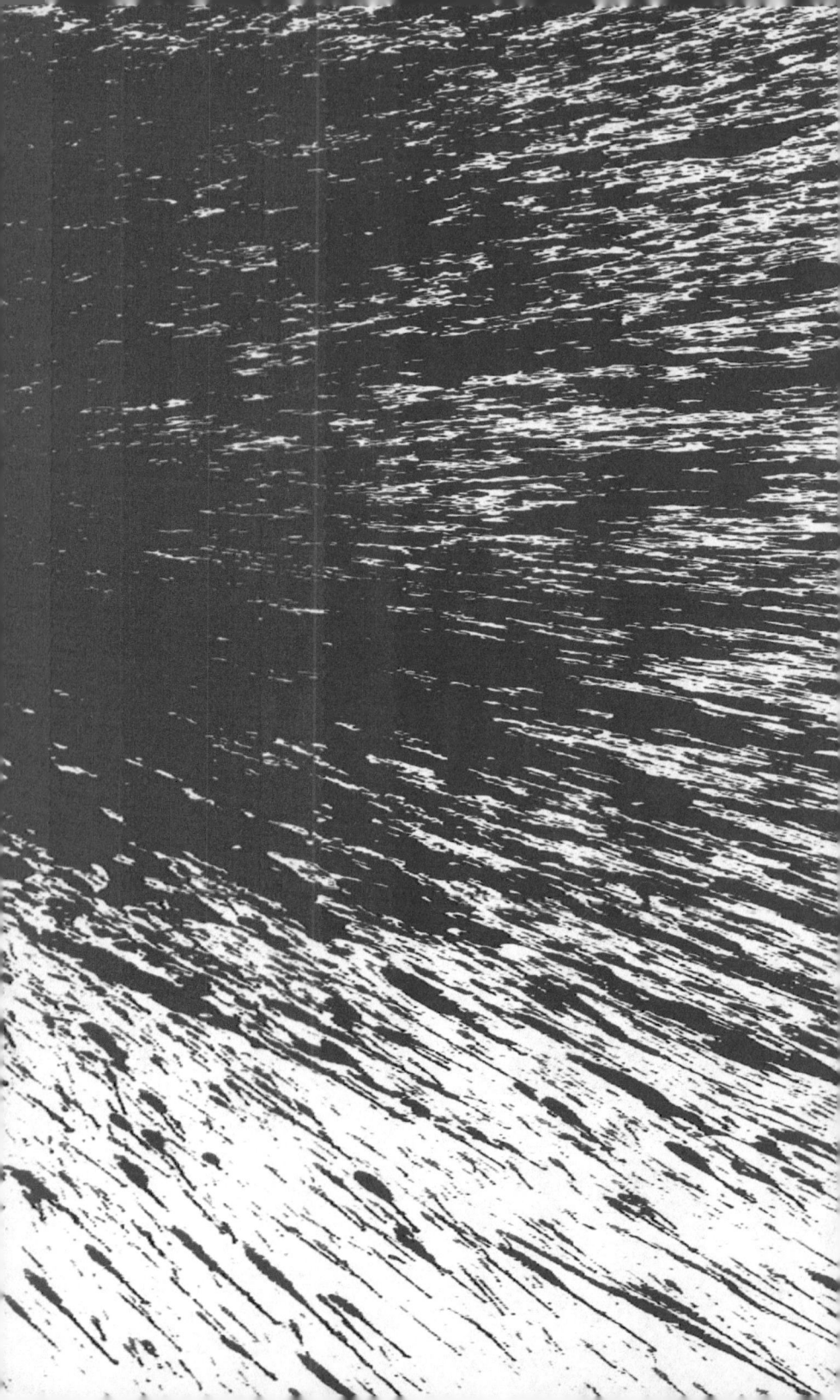

RUN, FRANK! RUN!

HE WAS RUNNING. THREE MILES FROM HOME, AND DEEP ON HIS USUAL ROUTE, BUT HE WAS GETTING MORE AND MORE FRUSTRATED. THAT DELICIOUS ENDORPHIN RUSH—THE RUNNER'S HIGH— ELUDED HIM.

He should have been soaring by now, basking in the heady euphoria, oblivious to his aging body. Today, though, he was just slogging along, perplexed and struggling. It seemed the Gods, smirking, had dialed up the heat of the sun and over-cranked the pull of gravity. He listened to the labored huff of his breath, felt the jarring tread of his footfalls. He winced at the fiery jolts knifing through his lower back. His sore calves and soggy tank top compounded the misery. He slowed to a walk and trudged along the paved jogging path.

A quick glance at his watch told him he was way behind time. He should be at the turnaround by now. He could at least see it up ahead, perhaps five minutes away, a large covered pavilion with a half dozen picnic tables huddled beneath it. The concrete path he was on wound through a secluded woodland park. The path followed the curve of a deep and placid lake. It ambled past a dilapidated marina, swept through a ramshackle campground, and made a loop around the weathered picnic area. He hurried his pace, despite the protest from his aching legs.

At last, he reached the cool shade of the pavilion and flopped down at one of the tables. He caught his breath. For a few minutes, he scanned the rustic scenery. Above him, the pavilion roof angled upwards to a high peak, where a single uncovered light bulb dangled from the ceiling. To his left, the lake shimmered blue and inviting. On the right, a thick stand of dark and brooding trees stretched beyond the neatly manicured lawn. Clouds slowly wafted across the sky. Birds trilled in the distance. A light breeze carried the husky scent of pine and damp loam.

He sighed, contemplating the long route back. The breeze picked up, caressed him, coolly whispering. As if to answer, he glanced along the curve of the concrete path and noticed a narrow dirt trail which snaked off across the lawn. The trail knifed through a gap in the trees and disappeared into the beckoning wood.

He had run this route a million times, but he had never noticed that worn footpath before. It should have been so obvious too, as it stretched across the grass like a raw wound. How could he have missed it? It hadn't been there yesterday. Or had it?

He continued to argue with himself. Surely, the run was over for today. The sensible thing to do would be to head on home. He would easily be back by late afternoon to enjoy a hot shower and a cold beer. Maybe he'd even chase after Margot and try to talk her into a quickie. Even after thirty-two… no, make that thirty-three years of marriage, the sex, when they had it, was still toe-curling good. He smiled at the thought of her freckled body and her flashing green eyes.

And yet, the bare dirt trail called out to him. It pricked his sense of adventure. Perhaps a new high, clothed in the seductive thrill of discovery awaited him. He thought about the rumors. Years and years of hushed whisperings about the strange things that sometimes happened in those woods. He chuckled to himself, recalling the childhood stories. He still told them to his own grandkids, teasing them out with hushed whispers and theatrical tones.

Ghouls, goblins, witches, ghosts. All fun and games. But the disappearances? Those tales were more disturbing. The Morris twins. The Johnson girl. Old Man Carter. A few others, too. Gone without a trace. Except for their clothes. In each case, odd bits of their garments had been found scattered here or there about the woods. A glove. A hat. A dainty little shoe. He remembered the seventh-grade history report he had written on Old Man Carter. Tom Carter had left before dawn one morning to go deer hunting. Packed his kit, kissed his wife, and was never heard from again. They searched these woods for weeks. Not far from this very spot, as he recalled, and all they'd ever found was Carter's old Remington .22 rifle. A single shot had been fired from it, and the breech was jammed on a second misshapen shell. Old Man Carter had jerked the bolt back so hard and so fast that he had practically pulled it clean off the stock of the rifle. Couldn't shove it back home in time. That was weird. Carter was known to be the best shot in the whole county back in those days. A crack shot from over a thousand yards, some said.

Alright Frank, he told himself, *think*. He pondered the situation. The sun hung low in the sky. He held up his hand, fingers turned parallel to the horizon, as a measurement between the sun and the Earth. Each finger width represented about fifteen minutes of daylight. Two hand widths between sun and horizon represented roughly two hours until sunset. Plenty of time to do a little exploring. Casting a glance to his left, he followed the even orderly lines of the paved walkway as it doubled back along the lake toward the familiar campground. To his right, across the lawn, lay the rustic trail, beckoning to him... calling to him... seducing him as it cut into the woods and wound out of sight beyond the trees. He pursed his lips, and shivered, as the thrill of discovery rippled up and down his spine. He took one last glance across the familiar campground, then with a shrug, he strode off the cement path. Following the dirt trail across the lawn, he plunged into the solemn forest.

As he walked, he gradually began to feel lighter, more energized. He broke into a slow trot, loping along at half cadence. He felt the light breeze stirring, heard the cicadas screeching in nagging singsong rhythm. He quickened his pace slightly. The trail led him deeper into the woods.

He padded along like this for a while. At one point, he glanced up through the narrow gap in the treetops, took note of the sun, dipping lower in the sky. A quick glance at the watch. It was just after 4:30 in the afternoon. *Still plenty of time to see where this goes*, he thought, and pushed himself further. He felt rivulets of sweat trickling down his neck. Low scrub brush along the edge of the trail occasionally scraped his bare legs. A strange urged gripped him, and he suddenly imagined himself in a Tarzan-style loin cloth, loping through the heart of a dark and nameless jungle. He abruptly slowed to a walk and asked himself an unusual question—Or was it perhaps the trees that asked it of him? At any rate, the thought vibrated at the base of his skull: *What would it be like to run barefoot?*

He looked down at his feet. He wore the fluorescent orange Asics that Margot had bought him. He pulled them off, along with his socks, and stuffed the socks into the shoes. He held them for a moment. Then he crouched low, gathered himself, and sprung upwards, flinging both shoes high into the air. One shoe arced out of sight and landed with a thump beyond a tangle of thick brush. The other shoe caught high on a branch and hung suspended by the heel. It perched there like a brightly colored bird. He stared up at the odd image of a neon sneaker hanging in a hickory tree.

A smirk rippled across his face, and a hysterical giggle burbled to his lips. All around him, he noticed again, the rasping thrum of the cicadas. They mocked him with their shrill rhythmic chatter. He listened closely, thinking perhaps he heard something else there. Words almost. A disturbing murmur emanating from deep among the trees. He shook his head dismissively.

He struck out again, this time at full stride. The trail carried him deeper and deeper into the gloomy wood. The ground felt hard and gritty. As his bare feet punched the dirt trail, they seemed to absorb the swell of life pulsating all around him. Birds sang in lilting riffs. The wind stirred the branches and aroused the damp, leafy aroma of the forest. Insects flitted among the wildflowers. A murmur, maddening, indecipherable, swelling among the breeze, mingled with the rasp of the cicadas. It formed a heady mix, making him feel strangely energized.

He ran and ran and ran. The runner's high, when it finally came, hit suddenly, with a force he'd never known before. Every sense felt over-amped. The notion of time melted away. He ran on effortlessly. He basked in the rhythmic sway of his body, and felt the intricate clockwork tinkering of the human machine which bore him along.

He imagined himself the offspring of a god. Perseus, perhaps, fleeing through the woods with stolen fire. He snatched up a heavy stick from the edge of the trail, and as he ran, he carried it like an Olympic torch. An ancient undercurrent swept him onward.

Gradually, the fantasy subsided. He slowed to a stop, surprised at what he was about to do. He flung the heavy stick into the trees and looked hurriedly around. His only companions were the cicadas and the sagacious old trees. He stripped off his soggy tank top and cast it to the ground. Then, impulsively, he hooked his thumbs into the waistband of his running shorts and gripped the elastic band of his athletic supporter. With a loud grunt, he yanked both garments down past his knees, stepped out of them, and cast them away into the bushes.

Except for the watch, he stood there naked. He closed his eyes, inhaled deeply, relished the musky aroma of the woods. He tipped his head back and stretched his arms to the sky. He stayed there a long moment, breathing deeply, still in disbelief at what he had just done. His evaporating sweat thrilled him. He shivered and felt a sudden rush of arousal. The entire forest seemed to breathe with him, as he welcomed the exhilaration. Again, the trees whispered to him. Suddenly embarrassed, he opened his eyes and looked around.

The sun had dropped even lower behind the verdant canopy of trees. The light took on cooler hues of indigo blue, and the streaks of sunlight stabbing through leaves began to dim. He looked at his watch. It still read 4:30 PM. *How could that be?* He tapped it with his finger, pressed it to his ear. Focusing in closer in the dim light, he noticed that the running tally of seconds had stalled out. The damn thing had stopped. *Seriously?* He considered whether to turn back.

Not yet, came the suggestion. Frank stared up at the trees. He fought off a creeping sense of dread. *The old stories are just that: stories*, he told himself. Old Man Carter, the Morris twins, the others were just victims of bad accidents, weren't they? There was nothing to fear here. And yet, the trail called to him. He felt that the woods, somehow, wanted him to stay. Something urged him to press on, to be one with nature, to see what it felt like to be naked in the woods. Before he knew it, he was off, back to the measured tempo of his typical jog.

Soon, the runner's high swept over him again. He felt euphoric. He glided along the trail, plunging deeper and deeper into the mysterious wood. After a while, the high waned. An ache began to filter through his churning limbs. His thoughts drifted to an art class he had taken once in college, to a textbook filled with pictures of nude Greek athletes on the sides of an Etruscan vase. He felt the ache creep up into his groin and suddenly realized why modern athletes wore jock straps. He laughed out loud, and the sound scared him. He suddenly felt very alone, standing on the trail beneath the silent trees.

He never brought his phone when he ran this route. He knew the run by heart, and he ran for time anyway. Then again, he normally would have turned around at the pavilion. From this deep in the woods, he had probably doubled what he usually ran, and now he started thinking about how he would get home. He judged the light, fading every second as it filtered through the trees. He could still see, with difficulty, but probably not for much longer. Soon it would be pitch black and he'd be lost, naked in the woods at night. *Way to go dumbass*, he scolded himself.

He picked his way back along the trail, until he reached the area where he thought he had discarded his clothes. He was moving slowly; his limbs were stiffening. Soreness radiated throughout his entire body. He thought of Margot. She too was probably moving about, breezing into the den as she poured herself a glass of wine and settled into her favorite chair. *Damn, I'm late. She's gonna kill me,* he thought.

The trees stared down disapprovingly as he searched for his discarded shorts. He groped about in the gloom. He caught a glimpse of fabric in a damp heap on the ground. Thinking it was his tank top, he shuffled towards it, and reached to grab it. The slimy feel of the stuff made him recoil. He snatched his hand back. It wasn't his shirt at all. He kicked away a discarded scrap of moldy, mud-encrusted canvas. "Gah. Shit!" he muttered. He stood and looked for a leafy bush to wipe his hands on.

It dawned on him then, that he had tucked his key ring into the little zippered pocket inside the waistband of his jogging shorts. He'd thrown away his house key. The car keys were on that key ring, and so were the cabinet keys for the office. Now he had no idea where his shorts were. What if he never found them? He pictured himself standing naked in the den, stammering an explanation for Margot.

He could hear her chiding him, and his heart sank.

He felt cold and deeply weary. Mosquitoes swarmed his bare legs. He swiped at them and slapped at his skin wherever he could reach. There were dozens swarming him at once. The sudden flurry of movement stoked his rising panic.

Something heavy shuffled through the bushes off to one side. It was huge, by the sound of it. He glanced over his shoulder, then the other… anticipating God knows what, lurking in the encroaching underbrush. Through the thick stand of trees on either side, he could only see dark tree trunks crowding close together. He backed away cautiously.

Again, a wild crash and the rustling of leaves in the underbrush. The hair prickled on his arms and neck. He squinted through the gloom. A large dark shape, sleek and low to the ground scuttled past, just beyond his range of vision. With a yelp, he turned and ran. He felt the trail beneath his feet and sprinted headlong, hoping to God he had picked the right direction.

He ran until sharp pains stabbed into his side. Gasping for air, he slowed to a walk. He looked back down the trail. Nothing pursued. Up ahead, the trail gradually widened as it led towards an open area in the woods. As he drew nearer, a prickling sensation crawled up the back of his neck.

He stopped at the end of the trail and stared about in hushed wonder. A clearing spread open before him, rounded and high roofed as an ancient cathedral. The trees, aged and unyielding, kept watch like giant sentinels. In the very center of the clearing, the sepulchral heart of the place, stood a gnarled stump, wide and solid, deeply rooted; an altar of sorts, shaped perhaps by the hand of some dark, preeminent being. The place vibrated with the hushed whisperings of long-forgotten rituals. The rustic altar summoned him—and he answered.

He approached obediently and knelt upon the damp earth before the timeworn stump. It was wide and knotty, stretching at least four feet in diameter. Its top was flat and worn smooth. He gazed at the growth rings as they spiraled in concentric circles across the ancient surface. They began to swirl and pulsate with life. The surface of the stump began to change. It was no longer solid wood. Instead, it grew dark, black as ebony—and deep as the abyss, like a portal to the depths of the earth. He felt a deep, bone-chilling cold, a hint of the infinitesimal vacuum of space, and a mind-numbing glimpse of the creatures who dwelt therein.

As he gazed into the shimmering blackness of the stump, the surface rippled like water and he saw the sudden formation of a dark shape, deep within. The surface began to boil, as an oily liquid oozed down the sides of the stump. He backed away, and the stuff gushed forth as a dark misshapen beast burst from the stump. The thing was huge, bat-like—and it was mewling like a wounded cat. It stretched to its full height, towering as high as the trees. Slowly, it flexed its leathery wings, and glared about with eyes like flaming coals. Frank fell back, terrified, crawling frantically away from the demonic creature. He scrambled away and hid behind a thick bush, unable to tear his eyes away.

As he watched, the beast raised its head, craned its neck, and howled, deep-throated and menacing. At its call, the shadows gathered and shifted, forming into black beasts, hunch-backed and simian, shuffling heavily through the brush, gathering in a ghoulish cabal, bowing to their master.

The huge bat-like brute leered about, sentient, hungry. It sniffed the air, turning its baleful gaze toward the scrap of brush where Frank cowered. His heart hammered at his chest. The thing huffed the ground, nostrils flaring at the scent of him. Panic rose in Frank's throat. And the thing screamed a high and piercing war cry, answered by the howl of the shadow beasts.

At that, Frank fled. He plunged through the woods naked, twigs and craggy brush scraping his arms and legs. He pictured the path to the lake, the path to the pavilion, the lay of the campground… and the way back to Margot. He had to make it back to her. He ran and ran and ran.

At his heels, he heard the snorting shadow beasts as they loped through the brush behind him. He sprinted harder, legs drumming like pistons, arms churning, swiping at branches. He dodged tree trunks, slammed into them, glanced off them in the darkness, trying to stick to the trail. He suddenly remembered the words of his college track coach, "Keep everything straight, boy, toes, knees and elbows. No wasted movement."

RUN, FRANK! RUN!

No wasted movement. He ran for his life, fleeing from shadows. It was sheer madness.

His foot caught and he stumbled headlong. He slammed against a tree and fell hard. A sharp pain stabbed at his side. He grabbed himself and looked. A jagged stick, as thick as his finger, had embedded itself deep into his flank.

"Breathe through it," his coach would have said. *Breathe and keep pushing.* The words compelled him, as he summoned the depth of his will. He stood and kept running long after the sounds of pursuit had subsided.

When he found himself gasping, squinting in agony, his side screaming for relief, he slowed. He fought the urge to bend over, succumbed, hands on knees, chest heaving, legs on fire, then forced himself to stand tall and laced his fingers behind his head. A primal urge kept him moving.

He yanked the stick free and cast it aside. Blood flowed down his side. He stumbled along until he found himself in a familiar part of the trail. From here, it was perhaps ten minutes more to the pavilion. He listened for the sounds of the shadowy beasts.

All was silent. As dusk settled, the shadows deepened around him. He pressed hard against his flank, felt the wet blood, a jolt of pain, and a surge of nausea. He gasped for breath. He wanted so badly to kneel, to rest, but he knew that the safety of the pavilion lay ahead.

He plunged onward with measured strides. His side was on fire. His footsteps padded in rhythm against the damp earth. He heard himself panting. From behind, sudden bursts of movement crashed through the foliage. His blood turned to ice as he heard the high lilting call of the bat-like brute. It swirled overhead, blocking out the last bits of starlight. It hovered high above and summoned its feral host.

The shapes pressed in upon him, flowing from the darkness of the underbrush. Frank cowered there, rooted in the black umbra of the bat demon's shadow. As the beasts gathered, Frank gagged at their sulfurous stench. They began to solidify, and they swiped at him with jagged claws. A beast snatched at his wrist and held tight. A jolt of hellfire burst through Frank's body. He cried out and jerked his arm away. Flailing, off balance, he fell to the ground and rolled out of the darkest part of the beast's shadow. The simian thing pounced, but as it left the darkness, it faded again to mist, and lashed harmlessly at him. It shrank back, snarling, to reform in the heart of the blackest shadows.

Frank clambered to his feet and fled. He thrashed about as he ran, stumbling over uneven terrain and fallen branches. Behind him, the creatures lurched forward in a murderous rage. As his legs pounded the earth, he remembered the pavilion, and the light bulb which hung there. Surely it would be lit by now. Perhaps the meager light would disperse the beasts, or at least trap them in these ill-fated woods. He must make it there… It was his last desperate hope.

RUN, FRANK! RUN!

As he ran, he became primal, naked, hunted, as panicked and fearful as a helpless rodent. He was driven by the thought of the dim pool of light that must lay beyond the edge of the forest. He saw the trees, just ahead, thinning. Beyond, the soft greenery of the lawn, and there stood the pavilion, silent and empty, bathed in the faint sputtering glow of the single light bulb. He bolted towards it, sprinting with all his might.

Even so, the last vestige of dusk faded out, and the night descended upon him. His footfalls churned up black wisps of smoke as a fetid mist swirled about his feet. The dark beasts lurked at the edges of his vision. He felt chills as their talons reached for him. Their master, the bat creature, swooped low and belched an oily sludge onto the ground at Frank's feet.

The stuff boiled up with a loud hiss, and the earth melted beneath him. He found himself falling, down and down, until he slammed hard at the bottom of a deep hole. He lay there for a moment, dazed, staring up at the night sky. The silent shadows slowly gathered above him. Before he could scramble to his feet, the simian things leapt upon him. He cried aloud, in agony, in desperation, in anger at being so close to freedom. Icy-cold talons knifed into him and choked his screams. The bat-like beast howled in triumph, as the darkness engulfed its prey and melted into silence.

◻ ◻ ◻

Two days later, scores of men in camouflage searched the grounds near the pavilion. Margot waited, huddled in the passenger seat of the sheriff's SUV, fingers drumming the sides of a chipped coffee cup. Past the edge of the pavilion lawn, the trees stood in gnarled columns without a trace of the trail that Frank had followed. The foliage waved gently in the breeze, an unblemished blanket of green, except for a single patch of blackened weeds. With no sign of Frank, and no evidence of any trail to follow, the searchers quartered off and tromped through the underbrush. Day after day, week after week, exhausted search parties plunged as far as they dared into the silent wood.

Eventually, they gave up, as they had many times before. The town grew quieter, and Margot moved away; some said she went to live with her sister out on the coast. With Frank gone, there was nothing left for her there. Despite the fliers, the phone calls, and the relentless searches, no remnant of Frank was ever found, save for a single sneaker—a fluorescent orange Asics running shoe, perched high upon the branch of a frail and withered hickory tree.

WE CAN EASILY FORGIVE
A CHILD WHO IS AFRAID
OF THE DARK; THE REAL
TRAGEDY OF LIFE IS
WHEN MEN ARE AFRAID
OF THE LIGHT.

~PLATO

MIDNIGHT SNACK

MIDNIGHT SNACK

THE SUMMER EVENING WAS HOT AND CLAMMY, AND THE URGE BECKONED THURMAN AS HE STOOD AT THE WINDOW OF HIS CRAMPED APARTMENT. THE RUSTED AIR UNIT RATTLED ON, USELESS AGAINST THE HEAT. HE WAS NEARLY NAKED, HIS ONLY GARMENT A PAIR OF DAMP LINEN BOXERS. HE PRESSED HIS SWEATY BROW TO THE HALF-OPEN WINDOW PANE, AS IF TO ABSORB THE LANGUID VIBES OF THE CITY STREETS FAR BELOW. THE URGE ROSE. HE FOUGHT IT, FORCED IT BACK DOWN, DEEP WITHIN. IT GNAWED AT HIM, STILL; AN ITCH THAT HAD TO BE SCRATCHED.

He scanned his reflection in the glare of the window. He was not a tall man, but he was solidly built. His nappy black hair was shaved down to a jarhead flat top; his rangy brown limbs bore the scars of his three tours in the 'Nam. Now here he was, home at last. A civilian. The war was winding down, and how long had he been back? A year? Thirteen months? He laughed aloud at the idea. His first 'tour' back home was nearly complete. Nixon was on a roll and would probably get re-elected in the fall. Thurman wondered if he should re-enlist, to see the end of things first-hand. The thought sent a chill down his spine. He stared at his calloused hands. He slumped into a chair. He stared at the walls. He smoked a Salem. There was nothing good on TV.

And the urge was still there. The urge to have a taste.

He would go out tonight, he decided.

Yes, he must go out.

Rising abruptly, he rummaged through the kitchen cupboard, cranked open a can of Beef Ravioli, wolfed it down with his fingers. He chased it with a couple of beers, then went to his room to gear up.

At the stroke of midnight, clad in camo fatigues, jungle boots, and a faded army muscle tee, he descended the back stairs. He strode across the darkened street and slid behind the wheel of a battered Oldsmobile Cutlass. He punched a worn Earth, Wind and Fire 8-track into the tape deck. He drove around the city, the itch upon him, humming to himself.

After a while, he spotted her, the most promising one of the night, in platform heels, tripping along like a baby gazelle. Bony shoulders and endlessly long legs protruded from her skimpy outfit. Cruising slowly behind her, he eased over to the curb. He whistled. She turned and plodded over to the car. He rolled down the passenger side window for her, and she leaned on the door frame, resting her ample breasts on scrawny arms. She was pretty, despite the ill-fitting wig, the caked-on makeup, and the cheap-looking pearl choker. Yes, she would do nicely, he decided.

"What you doing out so late, little girl?" he crooned. "Won't yo daddy be looking fo' you?"

His gaze lingered over her pouty lower lip, then followed the supple curve of her neckline. She smiled and tilted her head.

"I dunno," she replied. "Maybe you's my daddy."

"Girl, tonight, I'm yo daddy, yo brotha, and yo nappy-headed first cousin. Hop in!"

She did, and he eased the Cutlass back into midnight traffic.

Thurman produced the pack of Salems. He lit one, steering with his knee. He offered the pack to the girl.

"Naw, I'm cool."

She turned up the volume on the 8-track. She snapped her fingers and gave a little shimmy in rhythm with the horn section.

"I love this jam," she said, smiling.

He studied her hungrily. In his mind's eye, he saw what would become of her. He imagined himself wrenching her limbs, grinding his knee into the small of her back, reaching for her neck...

Irritated, he turned his eyes back to the streets. She had been saying something.

"What's that?" he demanded.

"I said, 'Where you from, sugar?'"

"Nowhere. How 'bout you?"

"I'm right where I wanna be. Same as you."

Thurman laughed. "You say that now. You might not be saying that later."

His tone had a strange edge to it.

"You got a name, little Miss, 'Where You Wanna Be?'" he continued.

She batted her lashes.

"What you wanna call me?"

He leaned over the center console, leering at her. He clamped a sweaty hand on her thigh. "How 'bout, Dead Meat!"

She squirmed under his grip but made no effort to remove his hand. Instead, she dug into her handbag.

She produced a compact, opened it, and began patting her cheeks with the sponge.

"That's—sure, alright. I been called worse, I guess."

"I bet you have! Yeah, I like that. Little Miss Dead Meat."

He laughed loudly and released her thigh. She edged away from him.

"Aw, come on, I'm just havin' fun," he teased. "Ain't you havin' fun?"

"Sure, I guess so."

They rode on in silence for several blocks. The girl looked Thurman up and down. She saw that he was handsome, in a rugged sort of way, except for his eyes. Something dark lingered there. His thick lips held a rueful smile, and his skin glistened smooth and glossy brown in the passing streetlights. Muscles bulged from his chest and arms. Her leg still twitched from his gruff hands.

The car was moving fast. Peering from the window, the girl scanned the filthy, deserted streets. She picked at her pearl choker, stroking it back and forth across the tip of her chin.

"Where we going?" she probed gently.

"I know a spot," came the reply. "Real close."

Thurman steered the car off the main drag, down a side street, and turned into a darkened alley. He killed the headlights, then the engine. He sighed deeply and lit another cigarette.

"Sure you don't want one?"

"Naw I'm good. I don't smoke," she insisted, fighting hard to keep her nerve. "So what we gonna do, sugar? You never told me what you like."

He tipped his head back and blew a thick cloud of smoke.

"I can think of a few things."

She scanned the alley. On either side, blank brick walls stretched away into the darkness. No back doors. No windows. Perhaps fifty yards away, a single streetlight sputtered off, then on again. She felt his eyes slithering all over her body.

"I gotta tell you," she began, "my man, Uncle Boudreaux. He don't like no rough stuff. Treat me right, I'll tell him to fix you up something special for next time."

Thurman blew another cloud and flicked the butt out the window.

"Who says there's gonna be a next time?"

The girl dipped into her handbag again, hand trembling. She withdrew a tiny brown vial filled with a pale viscous fluid. The stuff glinted in the dim light. She quickly palmed it and held it low beneath her thigh. Thurman saw it.

"What's that, 'shrooms? You like to party?"

"It's nothing. Uncle Boudreaux gave it to me."

"Uncle Boo-drow? Who the hell is this Uncle Boo-drow you keep talking 'bout?" Thurman scoffed.

"Somebody you don't wanna meet."

"Really?" He laughed again, then quick as a snake, he lashed out and snatched her wrist. The vial was still clenched in her slender fist. He pulled her across the seat until she was pressed close against his hardened frame. She met his gaze defiantly. The husky stench of him washed over her.

"Show me," he demanded. He began to pry her fingers loose.

She giggled with rising excitement, fighting to hold onto the vial. He had almost freed it from her grasp, when she lunged forward and bit down hard on his stubby fingers. He grunted and let go. The girl fumbled for the door lock and sprang from the car. She laughed and fled down the alley.

Thurman watched her run, haltingly, off balance and floundering in her platforms. He exited the car and bolted after her.

The girl looked over her shoulder, saw him gaining ground. She peeled off her shoes, throwing them wildly away, then turned again to run.

Thurman yelled after her. "Ready or not, here I come!" His blood was up. He broke into a dead sprint. In a flash, he had closed the gap. He shoved her from behind, and she tumbled hard onto the concrete. The urge was there again, pulsing hotly. He withdrew a combat knife from his belt. He held it out, so that it glinted in the dim light.

She began to cry, bear-crawling backwards away from him on hands and heels. At last, he stood over her. She raised her tiny fist defiantly, fingers gripping the fluorescent vial. She called out, in a strange sing-song rhythm, "Uncle Boudreaux, guardian of night, I call on you now, to make things right!" She slammed the vial onto the ground. It shattered to bits, releasing acrid smoke into the night air.

Thurman blinked hard, his eyes tearing up, his lungs on fire, as the girl scuttled away beneath the noxious fumes. Thurman rubbed his eyes. What he saw next surprised him. A man had somehow emerged from the dwindling cloud. He stood over the girl and helped her to her feet. He was black, strangely tall, rail thin, and regally dressed in a silk top hat and tails. His face was painted white, in the shape of a leering skull. He brandished a gnarled cane with a ragged, shrunken head for a handle.

"What's all 'dis now?" the man asked in a swampy drawl.

"He tried to hurt me," the girl cried. She pointed an accusing finger at Thurman.

The man smiled. He stood, legs wide, the cane firmly planted in the ground before him.

"Well, we ain't gon' put up wit dat—no, no. Ol' Unca Boudreaux came just in time, den."

"You run 'long den, now," he said to the girl.

She flipped Thurman the bird and shuffled off down the alley.

Thurman leaned back and laughed. "Hey dere," he called mockingly. "You gotta be fucking kidding me, man! It's a little early for Halloween, ain't it?"

"Don' be no foo', mahn," lectured Boudreaux. "Fuhget 'bout dis here li'l wahn. She ain't fo' you tahnite. Best be on ya way, den."

Thurman stood his ground. His prey was escaping down the alley. He heard her footsteps pat-pat-patting as she ran. The urge boiled over into rage. He brandished the knife.

"What the fuck do you think this is, man? Get outta my way or else."

"Else wha, mahn?"

"How 'bout I do you, right here. Right now. Then hunt that bitch down and slice her up. Two for the price a one. How's that sound?"

Now it was Boudreaux's turn to laugh, a deep chuckle that dwindled off into a weird snort.

Thurman lunged, thrusting hard for Boudreaux's liver. With lighting speed, Boudreaux's cane lashed out, smacking Thurman's wrist. The knife flew from his numbed fingers. Thurman gathered himself, unleashing a brutal kick to the man's groin. Boudreaux, with his bizarre, stilt-like posture, simply side stepped, then whipped the cane hard at Thurman's neck.

Thurman threw his elbow up at the last second. The cane smacked hard against his forearm, knocking him to the ground. In a flash, Boudreaux was upon him, grinding his knee into Thurman's chest, pinning him to the ground.

"Sumtin fo' yo' trouble, eh, mahn?" Boudreaux grinned. Then his body convulsed, and he regurgitated something slick and round into the palm of his hand. He held it up for Thurman to see. A single pearl, translucent, swimming in bile, pinched between his spidery fingers. Boudreaux laughed deeply, then moaned a strange sing-song chant. His eyes rolled back into his head, giving the full visage of a barren skull. Thurman struggled with all his might, but lay trapped beneath the gawky giant. Boudreaux stopped moaning. Then he took the slick pearl and shoved it into Thurman's ear. Thurman screamed in pain as Boudreaux's bony finger plunged deep into his skull.

Boudreaux rose to his feet and lifted his arms to the sky. A thick cloud of mist sprang up around him, hiding him from view. He laughed chillingly, and when the smoke cleared, he was gone.

Thurman wiped a chunk of phlegm from his ear and stumbled back to the car. He slumped into the back seat. He had a pounding headache. He felt dizzy, disoriented, and drained. He curled up on the seat cushion and sank into a deep and troubled sleep.

◻ ◻ ◻

Dawn lightened the sky as Thurman stumbled up the apartment stairs. He let himself in and collapsed on the couch. He rubbed his eyes. A dull sonic hum buzzed somewhere in the depths of his mind. A sudden thirst gripped him. He crossed to the refrigerator. Opening it, he scanned the jumble of tin cans and snatched a soda from the shelf. He gulped it down greedily, then gagged and spat a thick mouthful into the sink.

The strange hum grew slightly louder. It was now audible just below the volume of his inner thoughts. It carried a strange undercurrent, like the murmur of a thousand voices in a crowded theater. He felt a vague pressure on the left side, as if he had been swimming, and the water had collected there. Like that patrol in '69, when he had tumbled from a narrow rope bridge and had plunged into the river. The current had swept him downstream. He had to shed his gear to stay afloat. Crawling at last to the shore, he had to navigate nearly two miles back to the exfil point. He wriggled his lower jaw back and forth. The clogged feeling stayed with him.

He strode over to the couch, plopped down on it and hunched over the coffee table. He lit a cigarette, leaned back, blowing lazy curls of smoke toward the ceiling. It was then that he heard it, faintly, as if from a great distance. A high-pitched laugh. He rose, listening hard, scanning the shabby apartment. Again, seemingly from the bedroom, he heard it. A shuffling sound, as if someone were moving around in there. And the voice, now louder, a young girl, giggling, mingling with the strange humming undertone. That laugh, tapering off in the lilting, sing-song accent he had heard so often in the 'Nam.

The cigarette tilted from his mouth and fell into his lap. He brushed it to the floor and crept into the bedroom. He withdrew his knife and stood in the doorway. The shuffling sound came again, from the closet. The laugh rose, gurgled, and became a haunting wail.

He stalked closer, knife ready, senses alert. He approached the door and reached for the knob. The door sprang open, and he leapt backwards. A foul, dark cloud of mist broiled from the closet, and a girl crawled into the room. She was emaciated, dark-haired, and stank of excrement. A chill crept up his spine. She wore the tattered remnants of fishnet stockings. She stared through him with hollow eclipsed eyes. She reached for him, with long and gnarled fingers. He dodged her grasp and raised the knife. He struck violently, to bury the blade in her throat. As the blow arrived, the girl vanished. Having lashed at empty air, Thurman overbalanced and crashed to the floor. An echoing, high-pitched laugh crescendoed and faded away. He lay there, listening to his own heart pounding. The strange hum murmured in his ear. The rotting stink lingered.

What was that thing? The stockings, the sound of her voice... to his horror, he realized that he knew her. Or had known her, a long time ago. A world away, on a chance encounter in the back streets of Saigon. A drug fueled binge, a rotted mattress behind a dumpster, and with the dawn, she had become the first of those who would spend their last night on Earth, writhing in his arms.

Time spun away from him. He tugged at his ear, wriggled his jaw back and forth. He felt sick to his stomach at the thought of the Vietnamese girl, and then suddenly remembered the strange gem that had been pressed deep within his skull. It resonated somehow, throbbing, low pitched. He wrenched at it with his pinky finger.

He laughed at this; what would he do—pry it out somehow? He jabbed too hard, and a sharp pain jolted him. Withdrawing his finger, he stared at the tip, mushy with blood and yellowed pus. He staggered back towards his bedroom, and catching a glimpse of the clock, swore loudly. It was 9:06 AM. He was late for work.

◻ ◻ ◻

Thurman trudged into the warehouse like a convict heading to the electric chair. Guys went about their jobs, some ignoring him, others casting sharp glares. They knew what was coming as soon as Thurman punched the clock. No one wanted to be within earshot while Garvey, the foreman, chewed Thurman's ass.

Thurman stood before the punch clock and inserted his timecard. Right on cue, Garvey emerged from the office. Thurman bristled, fists clenched as Garvey stomped right up close. He was taller than Thurman, heavily muscled. His rugged butt-chin thrust forward in a disdainful snarl.

"You're late," he growled. His words slopped over a huge wad of chewing tobacco.

"Yeah," Thurman retorted. "So fucking what?"

The two eyeballed each other. Garvey inhaled sharply and spat brown sludge at Thurman's feet.

"So how 'bout I dock your ass, and knock you back on shit-can detail for the next two weeks?"

"Do what you gotta do."

Garvey leaned forward, jabbing a pudgy finger into Thurman's chest.

"Pull the forklift. I got ten stacks need moved, and don't be fucking sandbagging it!"

A frosty smile curled across Thurman's lips.

"You want that finger to stay on your hand? Or should I rip it off and shove it up your ass?"

Garvey jabbed his finger in even harder.

"Make that twenty-five stacks. No overtime. No breaks. And get it done or I'll fire your ass like I was lighting up a backyard barbecue. You got me?"

Thurman laughed.

Garvey looked him up and down with a grimace.

"Your old man's turning in his grave."

Thurman laughed louder.

Garvey shook his head and looked around. No one had witnessed the tense exchange. He spat, then strode into the office and slammed the door. Thurman flicked double birds at Garvey's backside, turned on his heel and stalked off towards the forklift bay.

❑ ❑ ❑

The forklift moaned like a wounded animal, but it churned dutifully along as Thurman steered it toward the loading dock. He steered carefully and directed the tongs into the pallet slots, cranked the levers to lift a stack of crates from the truck and backed away, turning a tight circle to steer his way towards the storage racks. The burly groan of the forklift helped him forget about the strange hum in his ear. The pressure and the ringing kept growing.

As he moved forward, shadows grew around him. The stacks towered high, obscuring the fluorescent ceiling lights, throwing eerie shadows. The forklift trundled down the row, and Thurman dutifully steered towards an empty rack. He cranked the lift, and it complained with a metallic whine, but the pallet rose, and Thurman guided it onto the rack. As he withdrew the blades, the engine sputtered and died. Thurman cursed venomously and dismounted. He raised the engine cover but couldn't see in the dim light. He would have to walk back to the factory workshop for a flashlight and tools. Irritated, he stalked down the dank aisles.

Returning with the flashlight and tools, he wound through the aisles towards the stalled forklift. He heard something scuffle in the dark. A blur of motion flitted past, skittering across the floor. "Fucking rats," he muttered. He flicked on the flashlight. Another scattered, then another. He saw them, fat and mangy, squealing loudly as they fled.

Something heavier shifted in the darkness. Startled, Thurman snapped the light to his left. A pale withered creature, an emaciated waif of a girl, crouched on her haunches. Thurman noted her pale skin, her bony limbs protruding from a filthy nightie. Her eyes glossy and black, spittle drooled from sharpened teeth.

"You see?" she hissed. "See what you did?" The waif rose to her feet and tore away her ragged blood-stained garment. She shuffled towards him, naked, arms outstretched.

Thurman winced at the sight, the once supple flesh, bruised, scarred, and rotting.

"You wanted me to play, so I did. Won't you play with me now? Like we did. In my mommy's room?"

Thurman's eyes grew wide in horror—in recognition. He gripped the flashlight, using it as a club, he swung heavily. The girl caught his arm in a dead stop, dragging him close enough to smell her rotted breath.

In an instant she changed. Her expression transformed to a look of utmost pity, as if a sense of regret could invade that immortal countenance. Somehow, then, as Thurman stood transfixed, he saw the skeletal mask of Uncle Boudreaux, hovering behind the ghastly pale skin of the wretched girl. A laugh, hollow, mocking echoed among the stacked pallets.

"See now? Dis here is de work ah de devil, and you's his henchmahn!" the voice cried.

The wretched apparition cocked its head back and laughed. Thurman yelped in panic, tore his arm free, and swung a mighty downward blow at the creature's upturned face. The heavy flashlight connected with a hollow thunk, and its skull cracked open, splattering him with something wet and mushy. Thurman felt the jolt run through his arm, and he winced, eyes shut tight against the pain. In a daze, he opened his eyes and stepped back, wiping slimy chunks from his face. Looking down, he saw that he was covered with the putrid guts of a shattered pumpkin. Rancid pulp clung to his clothes. Slick seeds and hunks of rotted shell lay strewn about the factory floor. The whole mess stank of sour rot. The creature was not there. Uncle Boudreaux's gleeful, mocking laughter rang loudly in his ears.

He stumbled from the dank corner of the factory storage area, emerging into the lighted entryway near Garvey's office. Garvey grimaced as Thurman stood there, mute and staring.

"Good Gawd, you smell like a sack of rotten assholes! Get the fuck out of here!"

Thurman made no protest. He simply stalked forward, stiff-legged and numb. His ears were ringing again.

Back in his apartment, Thurman stripped off his ruined clothes and stuffed them into a garbage bag. The sonic hum echoed dully within his skull. He crossed the short space to the bathroom, and for a long time, he stood under a scalding hot shower.

At last emerging, he dried himself and wrapped the towel around his waist. The ringing in his head intensified. He clamped both hands to his ears and felt as if he could claw his eyeballs out, if only to get at the resonant pearl.

In desperation, he stumbled to his room. He ransacked the small chest of drawers, his wallet, the pockets of his discarded jeans. At last he found it, a business card. He had accepted it, scoffing, months ago, when he had first returned from 'Nam. Now dogeared and hopelessly faded, he could still barely read the name inscribed upon it: Dr. Cecil Curtis, PhD, an army headshrinker, posted at the VA hospital on the near South side.

▢ ▢ ▢

Thurman sat in the lobby, staring at drab walls and sterile furniture. Nurses strode by occasionally. An orderly in a neat shirt and tie was working diligently taking surveys. It felt like he had been there for a long time. His head was swimming. His vision blurred, cleared, and blurred again. The sound of the resonant pearl grew louder—a concert of female voices, groaning in despair. He heard the echoes inside his head, and it disturbed him deeply. At times, a particular tone would rise above the swell, and he thought perhaps he recognized the voice. It reminded him of the times he had killed. Every so often, a word would rise above the din—the word *Why?* He searched his soul for an answer. None came.

At last, a nurse motioned for him to head upstairs. He trudged slowly, in a daze. Having reached the third floor, he walked down a long drab hallway. One door stood open at the end. A tall man, in spectacles and a starched lab coat leaned in the doorway, tapping a clipboard with a heavy fountain pen. His badge read "Dr. Curtis." He stared at Thurman, motioned for him to enter, then closed the door. The office was furnished like a comfortable living room, a couch, end tables, and an easy chair. Curtis reclined in the easy chair, tapping his pen. He motioned for Thurman to sit on the couch. He tapped his pen on the clipboard.

"Well," he began in a clipped accent, "what brings you in today?"

Thurman stammered for response. Should he have come? Where should he begin? What could possibly explain the weird events of the last two days?

"I— well, it's been strange lately."

Curtis scribbled a few notes. "How so?"

"Hard to say, just not—I mean, it's weird, you know? My ear. It's been bothering me."

Indeed, the low hum was there, pounding away at the back of Thurman's skull.

Curtis nodded. "Go on."

Who would believe him? This shrink, this lab-coated stiff he'd never seen before? It all suddenly seemed so stupid.

"And I've been, uh, seeing things."

"What sort of things?"

"Weird things, crazy things."

Tap, tap, tap went the pen. Curtis sat back and crossed his legs, the clipboard balanced precisely on his knee. "Can you describe these... things?"

Thurman sighed, then his words came in a sudden anxious rush.

"Is it true what they say, doc? That sometimes, you can be trapped in a dream and it seems so real?" Thurman rose and began to pace. He gesticulated wildly. "You go out and what you see, what you feel, what you hear, it's so real, like it's really happening. But at the end of the day, all you gotta do is pinch yourself, and you wake up, and it all goes away?"

Curtis sat silently, tapping his pen. He scribbled a few notes, then abruptly looked up. He gestured towards the couch. "Please."

Thurman shrugged and sat down.

Curtis leaned forward, as if arriving at something. "Have you tried it then, Mr…"—he looked at his notes—"Thurman."

"Tried what?"

"Pinching yourself, of course."

"Well, I…"

"Come now, Mr. Thurman. What you've proposed is an experiment. And a very interesting one at that."

"So?" Thurman wasn't sure where this was going.

"So, go on, try it. See what happens."

"You're shittin' me, right doc?"

Curtis tapped the pen. Subtly, the clacking sound swung into rhythm with the throbbing hum in Thurman's head. "I assure you, Mr. Thurman, I never 'shit' on my clients. You've presented quite an interesting hypothesis: that one may wake oneself from a dream. By pinching one's self, nonetheless. You should try it. Try anywhere. Your forearm perhaps."

Thurman looked perplexed. "This is fucking stupid!"

"Mr. Thurman, my methods may be unorthodox, but the results can't be refuted. Now give it a go. Or perhaps you are satisfied with your visions?"

Thurman considered this. Then cautiously, he took a very small pinch of his forearm.

Curtis frowned. "You call that a pinch? Mr. Thurman, I assure you, that meager effort wouldn't wake a fly, even if what you had proposed were true. I suggest you take another go at it. A serious pinch, for a rather serious fellow."

Thurman obliged, taking a large hunk of skin between his fingers and twisting hard.

Curtis began to laugh. He put a hand to his forehead in disbelief and pointed the pen at Thurman's arm. "You've really done it now, haven't you? Well, are you awake yet?"

Thurman looked down at his arm to find that a chunk of skin had been pried loose. It stuck to his fingers like a stringy chunk of bubble gum. Blood welled from the gash. Thurman gasped and scrambled off the couch. His ears rang in unison with Curtis's bizarre laughter. Looking down, he saw that his arm was whole again, as though nothing had happened. Curtis continued to laugh, doubling over. He rose and crossed to the desk, reaching for the phone.

"I've got to report this." Curtis picked up the receiver and dialed.

Thurman's shock quickly turned to anger. Fists clenched, he strode over to the desk and slammed both hands palm down.

Curtis wiped tears from his eyes as the call rang through on the other end. A muffled voice answered.

"Oh, you're gonna love this," Curtis laughed into the phone. "He thought he was dreaming! Just like you said."

Thurman gripped Curtis by the shirt collar.

"What the hell is goin' on!?"

Curtis held out the phone. "It's for you."

Thurman stood staring at the receiver. A deep, swampy voice echoed across the dull connection.

"What's all dis, now? You don' lack what ah've done? Ah'm showing ya who ya are, Mistah Thurman. You's the devil in black skin, you are."

Thurman lashed out, knocking the receiver out of Curtis's hand. He turned and fled from the office. Curtis's derisive snicker echoed from the walls.

In the hallway, Thurman struggled for control. His breath came in short gasps, his heart pounded against his ribs. His head ached from the throbbing curse of Boudreaux's phantom pearl. He leaned against the wall, head in his hands. He had to find a way to end this madness. Turning, he saw suddenly that the hallway stretched endlessly away. It was lined by countless rows of office doors on either side. He wasn't sure how to get out. At the far end of the hall, a tall, rangy figure emerged from the shadows. Boudreaux.

"You!" Thurman growled. "You did this!"

"Nah, nah, dat's de point ah all dis. You did it, suh, You. Are yah proud ah who ya are, Mistah

Thurman, proud ah what you become? An' shame on you, fo comin' after my li'l wahn."

"I'll fuckin' kill you!" Thurman snarled. "Get this thing out of my head! You get out of my head!" He charged down the hallway, past the endless pairs of doors.

Boudreaux stretched further away, like a warped image in a funhouse mirror.

"Yah, can'nah escape the past. Try as you might." Boudreaux gestured grandly towards the doors on either side. "You see."

Thurman grabbed the knob of the nearest door on the right. He shoved hard and it opened. Barging in, he found himself in the living room of the home where he grew up. His father stood there, drunk, belligerent. He knelt over a woman, wrenching her arm askew, digging his knee into her back, reaching for her neck.

"Nooo!" yelled Thurman. His father turned and looked with a leering grin of macabre triumph. He grabbed the woman by the hair and yanked her head around. Thurman stared into the eyes of his mother.

"Run Bobby," she pleaded. "Run away…"

Thurman shut his eyes tight, backing out into the hallway. The door slammed shut. He turned to his left, shuddered, grabbed another doorknob and thrust the door open. He stood in the back doorway of a liquor store, staring out onto a dimly lit parking lot. A single car was parked in the gloom, the windows were fogged.

Muffled sounds could be heard. Sounds of struggle. A boy's gasping sobs. The back door opened, and a man in a dark t-shirt climbed out. His pants were undone, and he fumbled to buckle them. Another man crawled out, wiping blood from his nose. He knew them both. They lived in the shabby tenement up the street. They slapped high fives and stumbled off into the darkness.

Thurman shied away, for he knew what was about to happen. A young teen emerged from the car, naked, crying. The young boy looked up, held out his arms in a pleading gesture.

"Bobby, it's me, Bobby. Won't you help me?" Thurman looked upon his younger self, crouched helplessly in the filthy parking lot. He turned his back and shut the door.

Thurman fled, looking for an escape. He plunged through another door and stumbled into the jungle. He tripped over a root and fell to his knees. A group of soldiers stood before him. On the ground at their feet lay a teenage Vietnamese girl. The soldier laughed at him, pointed to the girl. One of them called, "Your turn Bobby!" They stood cheering as if it were a football game.

Thurman struggled to his feet and backed away. The door shut. The cursed pearl thundered in his head. He stared down the drab row of doors. At the end of the hallway, Boudreaux stood laughing. "What else is dere? Do yah see who yah are?"

All the doors began to open on either side. Ghoulish

figures shambled forth into the hall. Dead prostitutes, slaughtered soldiers, the souls of his victims, dozens of them, lamenting their fate at his hands. And above it all, Boudreaux's mocking laughter.

The madness of it consumed him—the rousing sound of the pearl, the overwhelming sight of the dead.

"Yah know what yah must do," cried Boudreaux. And Thurman did know. He knew how to end it at last. He reached to the back of his waistband and withdrew the knife. He held it out at arm's length, every muscle taut. Boudreaux leered at him.

"Do it! Do it now!"

With a defiant sob, Thurman slammed the knife into his ear. Pain blasted his mind and he dropped to one knee. With a tortured scream, he shoved the blade deeper into his head. Red gore splashed down his shirt. He felt hot blood pulse over his fingers and the knife quivered in his hand. His head was on fire. He rose, stumbled down the stairs, burst through a door, and staggered into the barren alley behind the building. He collapsed to his knees. The blade jutted from his ravaged ear. Thurman clutched at the handle and pulled down. Jolts of agony shot through him as he wrenched the pearl free. He knelt there for a moment, exhausted, weeping. The knife fell from his hand. The pearl lay on the ground in a widening pool of blood. Thurman slumped face down onto the concrete beside it. He felt cold and strangely empty. He rolled over onto his back and gazed up at the night sky. The stars gleamed like gems on black velvet.

Gradually, a sense of peace settled over him, and a flicker of movement crossed his fading sight. He turned his head to watch as a dark hand with impossibly long fingers reached down and scooped up the pearl. Boudreaux stood there, one hand fondling the bloody pearl, and the other arm draped about the shoulders of a young girl. Thurman recognized her: "Little Miss Where You Wanna Be" in platform heels. She nuzzled close to Boudreaux's chest and stared down at Thurman.

"Told you ya didn't want to meet him," she scoffed.

Thurman watched as Boudreaux unhooked the pearl choker from her neck. With deft strokes of his gangly hands, he wiped the blood off Thurman's pearl and threaded the new orb onto the necklace. He clasped the choker back around her neck. He kissed her tenderly on the forehead and pressed a slim brown vial into her hand.

"Yah done de right ting by summonin' me again," he told her "Now dis one can leave dis worl' in peace."

Peace... Thurman savored the idea...

His eyelids fluttered closed. As he lay there, the urge slowly ebbed. He liked the feeling. He decided to keep his eyes shut, just for a few more moments. To rest—to rest in peace. Something dark and quiet settled over him. The world dwindled away to nothing, and deep within his tortured mind, the urge, along with the maddening hum of the pearl, at last, faded into silence.

ABOUT THE AUTHOR

Michael Julius Buckner is a high school administrator who lives in the Omaha metro area with his loving wife and family. A graduate of Northwestern University in Evanston, Illinois, he has enjoyed nearly thirty years in education as an English teacher, reading consultant, and athletic coach. He's passionate about comics, movies, and binge-worthy TV shows.